THE ENVELOPE

A COLLECTION OF VERY SHORT STORIES

Edited by
Stephen Westland
and
Helen Disley

Copyright ©2014

All Rights Reserved

AUTHORS' NOTE

The stories in this book are works of fiction. Names, characters, and incidents are products of the authors' imagination or are used fictitiously. Any resemblance to actual events or locales or persons, living or dead, is entirely coincidental.

The scanning, uploading and distribution of this book via the internet of any other means without the permission of the publisher is illegal and punishable by law. Please purchase only authorised electronic editions, and do not participate in or encourage electronic piracy of copyrighted materials. Your support of the authors' rights is appreciated.

Contact Stephen Westland via email at

stephenwestland@gmx.com

THE ENVELOPE

A COLLECTION OF VERY SHORT STORIES

A man finds a letter in his mailbox. A common enough occurrence every day all around the world of course, but in this collection of flash-fiction stories you will find a letter at the heart of an extraordinary range of circumstances including lust, betrayal, love, death, murder, desire and, occasionally, a hint of the unexplained.

Twenty-one flash-fiction stories, all connected by a common theme, are presented by sixteen different authors from around the world.

THE ENVELOPE

Introduction -

Structure – Clay Kindred

Returning Theseus – J. Mark Bishop

The One – Helen Disley

2128 CE – Ján Morovič

Copperplate – Paul Weston

Lust – Suzanne Grinnan

Veronica – Alexandra Gekousidou

Bananas – Keith Findlater

The Secret – Stephen Westland

The Outing – Rasheeda Azam

The Post – Debra Fayter

The Letter – Nathan Dunn

About the Incident – Paul Gledhill

Arthur – Helen Disley

Letters to Rainbow – Nessie Wilkinson

A Man Finds a Letter – Janet Wolfenden

Scenes of Love – Paul Weston

Red Dress – Seahwa Won

Thirty Pieces of Silver – Paul Gledhill

Adam and Eve – Stephen Westland

The Game – John M. Bishop

About the Authors

A Personal Message

Introduction

This is a book of short stories; very short stories. Flash fiction is a style of fictional writing of extreme brevity. Although it is not very strictly defined we have taken flash fiction to mean stories of 1000 words or less.

In this exciting project we invited contributions from writers that would be limited to 750 words or less. The writers were free to write about any topic but were given the prompt – a man receives an envelope with some instructions. The range of stories that we received was extraordinary and we present them together in this collection. We hope you enjoy it.

Stephen Westland and Helen Disley (editors)

Structure

Clay Kindred

An envelope with instructions inside was in his mailbox. Or so he hoped, walking the walk he took each morning, past the roses, left at the driveway and down the road a few steps. But today, as had been the case for some time, there were no new instructions. He walked slowly back to his house.

He sat for a few minutes, sipping his coffee, trying to suppress the urge to dwell on the delay. In the past, the instructions had arrived promptly at the end of the month, give or take a few days. Now, it had been several months since the last set came, and he was fearful that they had forgotten about him.

He rinsed out his cup and put it carefully in the sink, then went out the back door to begin his daily tasks. After washing the car, he moved the grey box from in front of the third tree from the end of the driveway to the front steps. He waited five minutes, then moved the box to the back of the garage. After ten more minutes, he moved the box back to the tree. He had long since lost the urge to open the box and check its contents.

Next, he walked into the woods behind his house and checked the traps. The first three were empty, but the fourth held a squirrel. He lifted the door carefully and released it, then re-set the trap. He checked the rest of the traps and then walked back to his house.

It began to rain. He took his bicycle out of the garage and turned right at the end of the driveway. After riding for 5.5 miles, he stopped in front of the old barn. He replaced the rock that he had left yesterday on the fence in front of the barn with a new one, and then headed home again for lunch.

He poached two eggs for lunch and placed them carefully on a blue plate next to three pieces of toast, and walked over to the refrigerator. He removed a large tin of olives and carefully counted out seven and placed these next to the eggs on the plate.

He closed the refrigerator door, but when he did this a piece of paper, which had been attached to the door with a magnet, fell onto the floor. It was the old instructions.

There hadn't been a need to re-read them for some time, as he had long since committed them to memory. Out of sheer boredom, he took them to read with his lunch.

Halfway through his lunch, his glass fell to the floor. He began to weep softly. Through his tears he cried "Six olives. Six olives. I'm sorry. I'm sorry." He took one olive off his plate and placed it back into the tin, then reattached the instructions to the refrigerator with the magnet.

He composed himself, then placed his dishes carefully in the sink and spent the afternoon finishing his routine.

The next day he went outside. The grey box was no longer in front of the third tree. His heart racing, he walked quickly to the mailbox. Inside the mailbox was a white envelope. Inside the envelope there were new instructions.

Returning Theseus

J. Mark Bishop

In the mailbox there was a solitary manila hemp envelope; he stooped slightly to retrieve it. The letter contained instructions summoning him to Westminster Magistrate's Court.
Theseus walks towards his second wife, Phaedra, reclining on the teal taffeta chaise longue, languidly naked under a translucent white sheet. In a knowing echo of Cabanel, one arm loosely dangles towards the floor; the other ruffles sensuous waves of long black hair. She is smiling, beguiling; then notices his frown.

"What is it, my love?"

"Now there's money at stake, she's summoned me to court."

"Why?"

"To prove I'm Theseus."

"And so this love deceives .."

Upon hearing the name, Theseus entered court.
    Neither side disputed that shortly after entry into Mars orbit the *Mars One* spacecraft was struck by the largest solar-flare events ever recorded, immediately killing three of the four crew. And that despite frantic efforts from mission-control, five years of

radio-silence accrued before this latter day *Flying Dutchman* reappeared in earth orbit.

The twin forks of the prosecution's case merely questioned how the spacecraft - widely billed as embarking on a seven-month one-way trip - could possibly have made it back to earth; and how Theseus could possibly have survived so many years alone in the remorseless silence of space.

The prosecution would deploy a recent paparazzi photograph - showing Theseus, leaning across an Acropolis restaurant table, slapping Phaedra's face - to expose this 'Mars Conspiracy'. In a series of old photographs the plaintiff, Hippolyta, Theseus' ex-wife, trenchantly demonstrated the defendant's left arm with a tattooed profile of Hippolytus, captioned 'Until the sea shall free him'. The left arm of the man in the infamous paparazzi shot was emphatically unemblazoned.

In their rebuttal, the *Mars One* team and Theseus' defence was straightforward: firstly, although lost to radio-silence, several tracking stations had unearthed verifiable records recording the progress of the spacecraft as it limped back to earth. Secondly, recently recovered video accounted for every second of life on-board.

As proceedings advanced the court watched time-lapse video of the mission. They observed Theseus entering the space X transit vehicle; the launch; the seven months of routine and then the extreme solar flare incident, which annihilated the craft's electronic communication systems and left three astronauts dead.

And they watched as, utterly alone, Theseus implemented his own Apollo 13 rescue plan; core systems were reprogrammed to force the craft to use its tiny fuel reserves to re-orientate itself for an improbably slow return to earth and he sealed himself inside 'Mars surface living module: No.1'.

And they watched Theseus pace his aluminium cocoon as days turned into weeks; weeks in months and months into years. Then, in rising horror and distaste, they witnessed the final stage of his voyage unfold...

Wherein Theseus busied himself with the ship's universal bio-reactor, seemingly culturing human flesh, bones and organs from stem cells extracted from his own olfactory mucosa. And then, in a series of increasingly dangerous and macabre operations, instructed the module's robotic surgical systems to replace, seriatim, his seventy-eight radiation-damaged organs with those precisely cultivated carbon-copies...

After the last video closed the District Judge Aethra adjourned the court to consider her verdict. On returning she quietly announced, "This court believes, beyond reasonable doubt, that the video and tracking evidence demonstrates a continuous time-line connecting the man who left earth with the man standing before us now; hence court confirms this man to be Theseus".

But as the verdict reverberated in the stillness, a man in the public gallery stands up and, shaking his tattooed left arm, forcefully proclaims: "Madam, I was once the man they called Hippolytus, lover of Phaedra; wrongly cursed by Theseus and cruelly drowned by Poseidon!"

"Four years ago, with my body lifeless in coma, Hippolyta reclaimed my father's organs from the *Mars One* mortuary. And finding no evidence of the radioactive damage which drove him to madness, she paid a surgeon to operate; to transplant each of my failing organs with those she had recovered: Theseus' heart for my heart; his brain for my brain; his blood for my blood. Then, as Shelley before, in her vanity she did command this body to rise."

"By your own evidence, my flesh is indisputably Theseus' flesh and the Telomere length of my cells tallies with Theseus' true age. So Madam, if you judge the defendant standing before you to be Theseus .."

Who the hell am I?

The One

Helen Disley

Saturday mornings were 'Tom time'. His wife of nearly eighteen years, Joanne, liked to sleep in after her usual Friday night out with the girls. Tom suspected his wife had not always been faithful, and at first it had hurt him deeply, but now he didn't really care. It was what it was and they both had to take responsibility for that. The truth was that Joanne needed Tom; and Tom – what did he need? Not Joanne, that was for sure, but life was comfortable, even enjoyable - just not entirely satisfying.

Tom took his coffee and warm pain au chocolat into the study, where the soft morning light was perfect for working on his sketches. He was behind with this particular commission and he knew he had to knuckle down and complete the collection before the end of the month.

A faint rustle from the hallway told him the post had arrived. "He's early this morning," Tom thought as he made his way to collect the morning's offerings. Just the one letter, a thick creamy envelope with one handwritten word on the front - 'Tom'. No address, no stamp. How odd. Not the postman then. He peered through the glass panel in the door but couldn't see anyone around.

Tom carried the letter back to the study, settled down in his favourite chair, slit open the envelope and began to read:

'*Dear Tom,*

I know this is out of the blue and totally inappropriate, but I ran into Paula a few weeks ago – remember Paula, my room-mate at college? We chatted about old times and it turns out she kept in touch with Sally, who married Dan, who of course was your best man......'

"Jesus Christ!' Tom turned over the page and saw the name he already knew was going to be there – Elaine. He stood up .... Elaine! He smiled at the thought of the beautiful, willowy blond he'd dated for over two years at college, the intensity of their relationship ultimately the reason he ended it – hating himself for doing so. He got up and guiltily closed the study door and read on....

'That's how I got your address.

When we broke up all those years ago I was a mess. I thought you were the one and it wasn't until I saw you with Joanne that it became real for me that it was over between us. Over for you maybe .....

So, I moved on with my life, not because I wanted to but because it was expected of me. I realised my dream of becoming a journalist, got married and divorced (twice!), I have a beautiful daughter called Anna and the two of us are the best of friends and look out for each other.

The thing is, the reason my marriages didn't work is because I never really got over you.... I thought you were the one........ and you were – you are!!

So now I find myself with time on my hands, with your address and all these memories, photographs, hopes and dreams, and I wonder...... do you ever think of me? Do you still love Joanne? Is there a chance for us now; older, wiser, damaged .....

The thing is Tom, you ARE the one. You always have been. You've been the inspiration for everything I've done. I knew it from the first day I saw you and nothing, absolutely nothing has changed.

So here's the point. I've gone to the Hillside Brasserie. I'll be there until 11am. If you don't come you won't hear from me again. I'm no bunny boiler!! I'll go back to my daughter and my career and my lonely life and try and forget that the man I love with all of my heart chose another woman over me.

But what if you come? What if you've been wondering if maybe I was the one after all?

11am ......'

Tom took a deep breath and ran his fingers through his hair. He sat down, checked his watch; 10:20am, and put his head in his hands. Finally he got up and put the letter through the shredder on the desk. He went upstairs and into the bedroom where his wife was still sleeping, unaware as she did so that her future was being decided for her; had been decided. A done deal.

Tom leaned down and kissed his wife on the forehead, moved a stray lock of hair aside, straightened the duvet.

"Goodbye Joanne," he whispered as he gently closed the bedroom door.

2128 CE

Ján Morovič

4am. Those pickup trucks come earlier every day. I better get ready. Whoa! Let's just stay down before my temples explode! How many shots did I have? It was Chico's stag night, or was it Diego's? Can't say I remember. Having Tequila shots wasn't the smartest thing in this heat. It's been like a furnace - no, a steamer! - for weeks now. I've got to move north. SoCal is not for me. Being a teetotaler and suddenly having, what six or seven shots, after a couple of bottles of Montejo and then something I couldn't even pronounce that Tito's uncle distilled at home (thank heavens I can still see!) ... Not very smart. I couldn't say no though. Chico - yes, of course it was Chico! - has been like a brother to me. When I had nothing, he shared the little he and Rosa could scratch together. And they never made a song and dance about it either. It was as if I had been their long-lost brother come back from a war. It was always: have another slice of meatloaf here, take some more mash there. Without them I would still be sleeping rough, or - worse - have to head back East and grow shareholder value. And I thought vineyards were about grapes! Anyway, these are my people now; this is where I belong! I may not know them all as well as Chico and Rosa, and the gang is different each day, but we all start at the corner of Maddison and 5th at 4:30am. If you aren't there at 4:30 you may as well not bother. And some days even that makes no difference. Only one or two pickups stop, looking for joiners, plumbers; trades that few of my confreres are au fait with ... Stop rambling, you fool! It's 4:06 and if you don't make it out by 4:20 sharp, you can kiss the 70 - or if you're lucky 90 - bucks that a day's slavery nets, goodbye. And I need that money badly! Kneecaps are at stake. Come on! 4:07am. At least the water is running today. Hallelujah! It's cold, but in this heat I wouldn't have it any other way. Not even with the thermo-piezo-servo contraption my father had imported from Sweden and installed in all the mansions' bathrooms would I need anything other than the coldest water on offer. Water - pure genius! I just hope there will be something in the shade today, and not because it is inside, deep underground or requiring a hazchem suit. I've had it up to here with cleaning crime scenes, or "processing" "meat." Becoming a vegan has never been so obvious. It is work though, and with people who have welcomed me among themselves. The knife edge that separates us from destitution may look pretty wide up close, even if it drives men to murder and women to the void. Ah, I can see Raúl and Pedro. ¿Que onda? Where's Chico? A job, where? The Chateau? ¡No manches! This will be awkward ... My father's conglomerate, of which his flagship vineyards are mere tendrils, has finally caught up with me. What a fool I have been to think that I could escape his Croesean wealth! Do I run? Or do I come clean to Chico, Rosa and my friends - no, family! - here? What will they do? Welcoming a homeless man on the verge of starvation is the most human of generosities, but an heir to the Morgenstern fortune who threw it all away? A man with nothing is one thing but I, who have left billions on the table, where do I stand? It was never about money though. My darling sister Beatrice took to the family business like an MBA to a venture capitalist, even my brother Charles, who at first refused our father's overtures, eventually joined the board. I suppose there is Daniel, who turned my father down point-blank and stuck to his guns, but at least he did it all in broad daylight. And I, where do I stand? My father never even asked me to join the company ... Was it because he knew I abhorred the idea of organized commerce, or did he not see that elusive entrepreneurial spark in me? All I got from him was a letter in my mailbox the morning I left. The day may have come to open it.

Copperplate

Paul Weston

He dreaded this time of day. *She* would be coming soon, dressed in her navy trousers and sky blue shirt, dragging that red trolley with the squeaking wheel. He shuddered slightly, his tired frame trembling momentarily. Every morning? Why doesn't she go to the next house? What had he done to deserve this ... this *torture*? He'd report her. Harassment! He'd have her struck off. No. That's doctors. Sacked! Yes – sacked. He stopped, an expression of surprise worked his face. Sacked? He half chuckled nervously, realising his inadvertent joke; giving the postwoman the sack.

Anxiety brought him back from his thoughts as the badly maintained front gate squealed. He gingerly squinted through the nets and grimy window. There she was, manhandling the heavy mail buggy up the step and on to the path. *Squeak. Squeak.* His gut twisted and he gritted his browned teeth with a whimper, driving his fingernails into his palms.

Leaving the trolley in situ she approached the door. He couldn't see. He had to see. He scuttled from the window to the living room door and into the hall. *Rat-at-at*! There it was – the old-fashioned brass letter box rattling back and forth as she pulled her hand back. *Thwap*! The letter hit the bottom of the empty box on the back of the door.

The old man shrank back, cowering against the wall, his face a picture of anguish and fear. As he fought to control his fear and straightened back up a picture dislodged from its hook and fell to the floor, the glass shattering into a million pieces. He whipped his gape-mouthed head round, shocked, looking at the fallen photograph – *a portent*? He knew the photograph even before he looked; he was receiving his pips, handsome, broad-chested, the policeman he once was. It was around then that he received the letter. All the others had been burned, save three. The first one had set it all off years ago. He'd investigated the death of the old man clutching a letter. He read it and later received one himself. He thought it a joke, slightly odd, but a joke nonetheless. Then the third arrived. He burned them after that. They took over his life; his wife left him, his family disowned him, he drank, he worried, he feared.

Forgetting himself, he stepped forward toward the old mailbox, extending his long-fingered hand. He swiftly knocked the lock mechanism aside and whipped his hand back as if bitten. The door of the box fell forward revealing the only item – a letter. Today was going to be the day, however. Today he would face his demons head on. Ha!

His shaking hand reached into the box and gingerly withdrew the envelope. Just the same as the last one: *Mr Peter "Chief" Elberg*, 24 Otterington Grove, Mulberry, was written in perfect copperplate handwriting, perfectly level, perfectly between the top and bottom edges of the envelope, perfectly black, a perfectly aligned stamp in the top right corner (equal distance from the top and right hand edges), postmarked for today. Always the same. Always precise. Today, though, that fine handwriting was not going to be incinerated. He was going to open this damnable letter and face it once and for all.

Shaking, he turned the letter over and licked his dry lips. His fingers caught up the unstuck corner of the envelope's flap and tore it upward. He slid his finger under the tear and worked a ravaged line along the fold. Stopping again to moisten his lips, the old man let out a rattling sigh, then reached and pulled the single folded sheet from the envelope...

"Hi Sarge."

"Penny! What you got?"

"Old man, sixty eight, lived alone. No helpers. No social. No signs of a break in. No marks on the body. Ex-copper!"
"Really? Okay. Show me."

Penny pulled aside the cover revealing the body, his arms and legs contorted at odd angles as if he had been trying to defend himself. His old face was twisted into a visage of abject terror. John Bowden frowned. "He looks like he was ... *frightened* to death."

He knelt beside the corpse to look closer. What's that? John noticed a piece of paper crushed beneath the old man. A letter? He straightened out the paper and read it.

The next morning several miles away at 41 Cockerton Drive an envelope, addressed in a fine copperplate hand, was pushed through a letter-box. It was addressed: *Mr John "Sarge" Bowden...*

Lust

Suzanne Grinnan

It had arrived earlier that day.

In the stillness of the city, laden with fourteen inches of new snow, he'd heard the mailman stomp his heavy boots as he'd walked up the old wooden stairs of the porch. He'd been out early, but not too, knowing neighbours were likely enjoying the extra hours afforded by closed schools and offices. Still, the sense of responsibility to clean the sidewalk weighed heavy on him — his grandmother's voice of civic duty repeating in his head — countering his need to be a good neighbour and not disturb the silence of the morning. A silence that only snow brings. No cars, no trains, but other unmistakable, precise sounds. The squeaky crunch of boots. The scrape of flimsy metal across pavement. Plastic dislodging ice from a windshield. Crisp voices in the cold air. Calls of camaraderie from neighbours experiencing communal purpose, a rare opportunity to connect over shared labour.

He'd heard the postman climb the stairs, but not the tell-tale clank of the letter box shutting. And so he'd gone out to ensure no errant flakes churned up by the wind turned mail to mush. He was attentive. A measured man. A man who considered all options *ad nauseam,* often driving himself crazy in the process.

It had been so with the catalogue. Page after page of luscious images. Plump, full, mouthwatering, with promise of abundance and pleasure. He'd earmarked them, circled options, made lists, crossed out some, added others, totalled the cost (with shipping, of course), questioned spending so much, tried to delete some, but couldn't imagine depriving himself for such a small sum (if one thought about it that way).

And now they'd arrived. A thick golden envelope too big for the letter box. Bulging, like a lumpy pillow. Sounding like an Aztec rain stick. Not something to be opened with a hurried rip like the water bill and plea to fund a local homeless shelter he also held his hand. No, this envelope held anticipation, the kind you took your time opening.

He placed it in the centre of the kitchen table.

Tossing the rest of the mail into a basket on the counter, he filled the worn copper kettle, placed it on a high flame, took down a tea pot — he had quite a collection, but this one was a favourite, admittedly fussy and kitsch, he'd bought it in Italy and the bright yellow lemons and vine turned handle lent a festive air to the undertaking — and then brought out another favourite, Earl Grey.

As the water came to a boil and the tea steeped, he kept glancing at the envelope and out the window in front of which the table stood. The window was rather small, with a thick, dark moulding. As he moved about the kitchen or sat at the table and moved his head, he created tableaus of the world outside, changing the angle to best fit the narrative in his mind. Sometimes his pictures included dogs or rabbits; sometimes the old man who walked the back alley. More often than not, they focused on a patch of dirt, not more than three meters square, now covered by dimpled snow.

Tea ready, he sat cupping a mug and looked out, then down. Here they were.

He opened the envelope.

Removing each packet he whispered the words aloud. Pearly Pink. Orangeglo. Bull's Blood. Tartar of Mongolstan. Isis Candy. Malakhitovaya Shkatulka (this one sounded out syllable-by-syllable, repeated twice as his tongue found more comfort with the sounds). Black Krim. Red Malabar. Trail of Tears. Ararat. Kabouli Black. Green Zebra.

He laid each one individually on the table. First in one sequence, then another. Like an odd game of patience, or solitaire.

Isis Candy. Pearly Pink. Black Krim.

Red Malabar. Bull's Blood. Orangeglo.

Tartar of Mongolstan. Malakhitovaya Shkatulka. Trail of Tears.

Green Zebra. Ararat. Kabouli Black.

Arranging. Rearranging. Back and forth. Up and down. Imagining how each would look as seedlings in this window, newly planted in the earth, bearing fruit, ripening, in a garden basket, and now in a colander under cool water, cut and salted, diced and sautéed, pureed into a rich sauce, roasted, canned, served beside a bed of lettuce, sliced on a baguette, atop fresh pasta, but best of all, fresh off the vine, warmed by the sun, bursting in his mouth.

Veronica

Alexandra Gekousidou

A man opens his mailbox to find an envelope containing a set of instructions.

> **FIRST:** *Find the blue house with the red door in Via dei Caduti.*
> **SECOND:** *Spot the anthropoid creature and chop off her head.*
> **THIRD:** *Remove the snake-shaped golden necklace and bring it to me.*

Bahia.

Luca folds the piece of paper and puts it back into the envelope. He has already been to Pavlopetri and he has also met the target - Veronica- before; very common in his profession.

What he recalls from their first meeting, is her look. He had emerged in her darkened eyes and the lyrics of a song echoed in his head: "Oh who will find me in your midnight eyes…?" They wandered around the paintings in the dark bar, named Bord dell'eau, but all he wanted to do was grab her and make love to her. He had been in a serious relationship for three years at that moment and he was feeling that it had become a wooden coffin, suffocating him. Angela was a real angel, whatever his mother had hoped for him. But that creature awakened new feelings he never knew he had. To him she was different, she was something else! He met her again, wanted to swallow her, got addicted to her. One night while kissing her, he felt he wanted to eat her alive. Crazy passion, wild feelings, with no release though. He had lost his mind over her! Lust…desire… Finally, he decided to move in with Angela, like everyone expected him to. He got himself a sporty motorbike; he felt he needed a change - and decided never to see her again.

Luca is a thin, tall man in his thirties, with ginger curly hair. It is cut very short with some locks going down his big forehead. He has round glasses, freckles and a beard. He is a cynic, saying that when he dies he doesn't even want a coffin: "Just bury me in the ground to be closer to worms". He doesn't believe in love or emotions and bull... Besides, Angela is now expecting their first child.

It is now evening in Pavlopetri and it is drizzling. There is heavy traffic and the sounds of a big, busy, hectic city echo in the distance, but the closer he gets to Veronica, the more the noise fades away and he gets surrounded by silence. His black, tight fighting clothes make it even harder for him to breathe. An old man, wearing a long, white cloth, approaches him with terror in his eyes. He looks like a wizard or a sorcerer. Luca notices a tattoo on his hand, which has the same shape as the necklace he had to bring back to Bahia. He pushes him away and the old man falls down and starts singing psalms. Luca shudders but moves on, and quickens his step.

Via dei Caduti. The blue door is unlocked; he pushes it gently and soon finds himself in front of Veronica. She and Bahia had been friends and partners for years and the golden snake was the symbol of their company; but Bahia had become very competitive and greedy. Besides, it is a truth universally acknowledged that the more there is evolution in an era, the more there is decline of moral values. Veronica's green skin is covered in a blue, long cloth, which embraces her curvy, feminine body. Her blue hair is down and she is facing the window.

She turns round and her golden necklace is glowing. She puts him inside her almond shaped eyes. He freezes, as if his feet were turned into stone. He goes closer and grabs her like a thirsty man does with water. He starts drinking like crazy, kissing her everywhere like a mad man. She isn't scared, only calmly tolerates him. Surprisingly, his passion turns into despise, his eyes fill with hatred and he throws her to the floor. Even this is veiled worship, but it confuses his judgment. He puts his knife down her throat with a fast move. Suddenly, he starts screaming and crying helplessly. The sorcerer gets in his room, singing the psalms to save his soul. Poor Luca! He's chosen to torment himself forever, because seriously, can you really ever get over such a love? Would you?

Bananas

Keith Findlater

I jumped as paper crashed onto the floor. Jumbled free newspapers and takeaway food flyers disguised the lack of any meaningful personal mail. All is good: no bills. Amongst this rubble was an unaddressed padded orange envelope. It felt crunchy and sounded gristly - hope it isn't a bomb. I opened carefully to reveal a colourful sachet of seeds illustrated with spotty bananas growing underneath palm trees.

There is a knock at the door.

"Hi George!"

"Hi Jack - hold on a mo'."

I pick up the mail to let him in and Jack spots the seed packet.

"You're not trying to grow bananas, it's freezing outside!"

I chuckle. "It says here that these seeds grow into dwarf banana trees!"

"This is Yorkshire, not the Caribbean!"

"I did see on television that someone is growing bananas in North Wales."

"It's always raining there!"

"Something to do with the warm Atlantic current, it's good for growing bananas."
"I bet they won't grow here."

"I reckon I could grow them indoors, it's warm inside with lots of light…"

Four months later, with much watering, six potted palms basked in cool sunlight with green leaves unfurling. I cultivated my green fingers by listening to the radio and extracting juicy nuggets of wisdom from Gardeners' Question Time.

"Dwarf banana trees need big pots!"

The plants grew.

At Christmas, Jack and his partner Melanie popped by and we got merry. They sung "Yes, we have no bananas!"

"If you use wheelie-bins as pots, it will give the roots enough space to help the plant fruit."

"It will weigh a ton with all that earth and compost."

"Just you wait, I'll have bananas growing..."

Later that evening, I found a bunch of bananas lying under the plants.

"That's the only bananas you'll get off those trees!"

By Easter, palms almost touched the ceiling, turning my living room into a tropical plantation. I noticed the floor starting to bow under the six green wheelie bins. I hoped the seeds were not mis-labelled as I didn't want coconuts dropping on my head!

Summer was hot and finally tiny bananas appeared. I showed Jack and Melanie in triumph.

"Jack got a packet of seeds through the letter box the other day."

"Have you planted them, you might get bananas too..."

A few weeks later, Melanie looked concerned. "Our seeds have grown into a plant that's already three feet tall."

"That's fast! Are you using plant feed?"

"No, but what is weird is that it shimmers when I water it."

"Shimmers?"

"Yes, and it moves too!"

"You're kidding!"

"No I'm not kidding, it shimmers and moves when I water it!"

"You're having me on!"

"No I'm not! But it's getting big so quickly."

"Can I come and have a look?"

"Sure, do pop round…"

"That doesn't look like a banana tree to me."

"Watch what happens when I water it."

Melanie used a red watering can to give their plant a drink. The pot's saucer quickly filled up then the water rapidly disappeared, reabsorbed with a faint sucking sound. The plant shimmered and drops of moisture dripped from its leaves.

"It seems to be perspiring."

"Look Melanie, there's a new shoot sprouting that is nearly touching the ceiling."

"What did the seeds look like?"

"They're tiny and they glow orange and purple in a pulsing fashion."

"That sounds dodgy!"

"Jack is down in the garden shed, we can show you."

The seeds on the wooden table pulsed with neon light like fireflies. They were hypnotic and I had to look away. As we returned to their house, we saw the shed glowing in fading light, mesmerizing moths and insects too.

We turned but the plant wasn't there.

"It's moved."

"It can't have."

Melanie slipped on a banana skin but kept her balance.

"Mind that banana skin!"

"We don't eat bananas, they are too fatty."

"Have you moved the plant, Jack?"

"No, it's gone!"

We searched the house and knocked on neighbours' doors but couldn't find the plant.
    Back home, I found my front door open and slipped on a banana skin. A strange shimmering noise came from within.
    Quietly, I tiptoed and peered in to see a giant plant amongst my plantation with baby bananas scattered all around my living room.
    I called Jack and Melanie. "Quick, come round here, I've found your plant!"
    We all gaze at the plants in wonder and disbelief.

"That's amazing! All this from seed packets delivered through our letter boxes."

The Secret

Stephen Westland

Jon parked his sports car on the drive and almost jumped out, such was his excitement to check his mailbox. The lady on the telephone this morning had promised him that when he got home tonight the package would be waiting for him. He ran to the door, his eyes fixed on the blue box that was attached to the brickwork just to the left of his front door. It was hard to believe what was inside waiting for him; or at least, what he hoped was waiting for him. The problem was that it was impossible to tell whether anything had been delivered without opening the box. Well, that was not entirely true. Sometimes a letter or parcel was too big for the box and the end could be seen protruding from the flap at the top, so that it did not close properly. This usually happened when it was his birthday, and also when he ordered a book online. Annoyingly, it also happened when he received over-sized junk mail items. Today there was no such protrusion, so there was no way to know whether he had received any mail at all.

He reached inside his jacket inside pocket and fumbled for his keys. The key that opened the mailbox was a small one, with a yellow plastic cover at the non-functioning end. Yellow was his favourite colour. He manipulated the bunch of keys with the fingers of his right hand to isolate the mailbox key from the many others on his key ring. The keys slipped from his fingers and fell with a clatter on the red tiles that covered the area directly in front of his door.

"Damn," he thought to himself and he bent down to retrieve the keys. He was just about to start rotating the keys again when this time the yellow key almost popped out and nestled nicely between his thumb and index finger.

His excitement and nervousness was in part caused by the cost of the item that he was expecting. He had paid exactly fifty thousand dollars for the advice that the company had guaranteed would change his life. It was three weeks ago when he had asked his colleague at work, Joseph, how come he was so happy all of the time despite the stress they were currently under with the redundancies. Over a drink that evening Joseph had revealed his secret. He had responded to an online advertisement from a company that promised satisfaction; the secret to eternal happiness. Bizarrely, the only way to contact the company was by telephone but over the course of several days and many telephone conversations the lady from the company had convinced him that they could deliver on their promise. He was sold on the idea. He had baulked at first when she told him the cost. However, as he told Jon that evening, what was money worth if he was not happy? Wasn't happiness worth any cost? Jon had taken less convincing because he saw the evidence in front of his eyes.

He asked Joseph whether he had regretted the purchase and Joseph emphatically replied, "Never. Not for one second."

Jon paid his money the following day and waited. Each morning he would come downstairs and check the mailbox even though he knew that it was too early for the scheduled deliveries. For the first week he had stayed at home until the post had been delivered which meant arriving late for work. Each day brought more disappointment; each more intense than the last. Eventually he stopped waiting for the post but would rush home after work to open the mailbox and inspect its contents. The last week he had spent many hours on the telephone talking with the lady from the company. She assured him that the package was on the way. This morning she told him it would arrive today. She promised.

He opened the mailbox and his heart stopped when he saw a single red envelope. It was addressed to him in golden flowery writing. There was no stamp. He opened the envelope carefully. The last thing he wanted to do was to rip the contents. Inside was single piece of paper with just one sentence written on it. He quickly checked the other side of the paper but it was blank. He read the instructions several times and then he started to laugh. Now he knew why the package had been so expensive.

The Outing

Rasheeda Azam

Charlie places a golden pancake, covered in plump blueberries, in front of Melissa and says, "Happy birthday love." His voice is strained and his heart thuds for no apparent reason. How had it come to this? Waking up scared, stuck in the flat all day too afraid to leave, and unable to sleep due to night terrors. He'd taken all the counsellor's advice but he didn't feel any saner.
Melissa stares at the plate as if it's covered in slop and tears fill his eyes. He blinks them away determined not to let her see more of his weakness. He looks around the pale elegant kitchen – at the shelves of cookery books and their crockery displayed on the dresser – anything to distract his mind.
"I'm late," Melissa says.
He turns and catches her glaring at him – at his grubby dressing gown – with distaste. She strides through the kitchen, her heels striking the wooden floor, her figure slim and stylish in a pencil skirt and blouse.
He rushes after her saying, "You haven't eaten breakfast."
She's halfway out of the front door before she looks at him with that mixture of exasperation, incomprehension and pity, and says, "Try and do something constructive today."
He's about to reply when the door to the flat opposite opens and he shrinks back inside, unable to face their neighbour. Melissa tuts, pulls the door closed behind her without saying goodbye, and heads off to work.
Back in the kitchen Charlie clears away the breakfast dishes while Mozart drifts from the radio and soothes him. His heart rate has slowed to normal and he vows that when his wife gets home

there'll be a birthday dinner and a present waiting, just like the old days: just like last year.

After cleaning the kitchen, he drinks a third cup of chamomile tea, does his breathing exercises before going to the bedroom where he dresses in jeans and a t-shirt. He sees that it's eleven-thirty – an hour after the postman delivers – and knows that if he doesn't go down to the communal mailbox now, to collect Melissa's present, he never will. He walks confidently through the flat, like he used to when leaving for work before any of this madness started.

But as he yanks open the flat door a dozen fears rush in and accost him. What the hell is he thinking? Anything could happen out there. He might bump into someone in the hallway? If they stop to talk he'll be trapped. They'll notice the shaking and the sweating. They'll think he's a lunatic. Maybe he'll trip up and go flying over the banister? Or he'll collapse and be unable to get up? His lungs are so small and tight he can hardly breathe, and he's about to spiral into blind panic.

But he remembers what the counsellor said about breathing deeply. If he doesn't collect the post there will be no present laid out for when Melissa gets home. Then she'll definitely leave him. He'll be alone in the flat. In the world.

He'd ordered a large bottle of her favourite perfume online: he'd wanted to buy her a diamond bracelet and necklace but she'd only complain about the cost as he hadn't worked in six months. There'd be a food delivery that afternoon – with champagne and flowers – but thankfully he had an arrangement with Waitrose where they delivered right to the flat door. Stepping into the hallway, he goes in freefall. He can barely see straight and his bowels have tied themselves into knots. But he makes his legs move one in front of the other until he gets to the stairs. How is it that his heart can beat so hard without rupturing? Grabbing the handrail he shuffles down three flights of stairs.

He approaches the large ornate entrance door staring at the basket under the letterbox that catches the post. There's s no jiffy bag in it large enough to hold a bottle of Chanel. The only item in there is a missed delivery card from Royal Mail. He'd calculated that the package would definitely fit through the letterbox. He snatches it up and reads it. The card didn't even give a reason for the package not being delivered: just instructed him to collect it from the local post office or request a redelivery tomorrow. Through the glass he sees someone approaching and rushes back upstairs, choking back tears over Melissa's birthday surprise being ruined.

The Post

Debra Fayter

The post always came at 9am. Not ten to or quarter past, exactly 9am. How, especially these days, the postman did it, Simon never understood. The old guy looked like he'd barely make it through his round, let alone be so punctual. Simon had followed his own usual routine and was waiting. He'd got up, checked email, showered and trimmed the beard his wife Sarah so disliked. 'It makes you look old' she always said. Simon was rather fond of it and anyway he was, if not old, at least into middle age. There were definite tufts of grey in the beard and that wasn't the only sign of advancing years. He glanced down at his expanding stomach. The gym would have got rid of that if only he could still afford the membership.
He wondered about returning to the computer ready to look for more opportunities. At least he could keep one step ahead when the post brought the usual rejections. In the beginning he'd focused on jobs in his field - telecommunications, and when that didn't bear fruit he'd moved on to general admin, then shop work. The rejections kept coming. There were three this morning by email along with the usual requests to take out a loan or to play online poker. He particularly liked the rejection from 'Bargain Books'. 'We had a large number of highly qualified applicants'. Christ, he could read, what more did they want? Simon wished he could tell the truth on application forms. 'Overweight, bearded, middle aged guy seeks a job to pay bills. Kind, affable, will do anything and be bloody grateful for it.' Lately Sarah's face had shown more worry. 'We really need you to get some work soon, it's nearly Christmas.'
The post dropped through the letter box. Alongside the bills was a letter addressed to him, Mr Simon T Nicholas. He opened it

straightaway to get the rejection over and done with. There it was. 'We are sorry to let you know that we are unable to offer you the post of Sales Assistant at Garnetts.' He stopped reading. What was the point of continuing with all their explanations as to exactly how he was deficient? He would return to the computer and try to forget Sarah's words this morning as she left for work. 'Look, it's November now, see if you can find anything so I can get the boys their Christmas presents. Harry really needs a new bike. He's grown out of the old one. Eddie's fixated on a guitar.' 'I promise I'll get something' he'd replied, unable even to convince himself. He'd always loved children. Running the cubs had stopped him going stir-crazy after the redundancy. He smiled. Making Harry or Eddie happy would be worth time spent in a rubbish job. He'd keep looking.

Simon picked up the letter to file it with all the other rejections. The second paragraph caught his eye. This was an odd rejection. 'Although we cannot offer you a role as Sales Assistant, we think you would be very suitable for a temporary vacancy that has just become available to start as soon as possible. If you are interested please ring Mr Gardener on the above number.'

Simon pictured Harry's face as he saw the bike. He could see Eddie strumming his first chords on the guitar. He pictured all the children's faces as they saw him. 'Costume supplied' the letter said. They wouldn't need to pad out his stomach too much, although the beard wouldn't be convincing enough..... He smiled as he dialled the number to accept this offer. It was a start. He couldn't help but let out a 'Ho ho, ho!'.

The Letter

Nathan Dunn

I heard the letter box clatter as it closed. I walked slowly to collect the usual letters from my bank telling me about how much debt I was in. The bank kept pestering me about this and I was SO enthusiastic to read about it, not!
Today there were three letters waiting for me. I sat down in the living room to open them. The first one, to no surprise, was a letter from the bank; I quickly tilted it horizontally and tore it down the middle. The second letter was from Dogs Trust telling me about how the dog I sponsored, Buster, was doing during the summer holidays.
However, the third letter was the one that shocked me. As I opened it I noticed how scribbled the writing was, as if it was written by a child, or as if someone was in a rush. There were three words written on the front of the piece of paper inside. They were 'Turn around NOW'.
At first I thought it was some kind of joke, but then I had the urge to turn around. It's like when someone tells you not to think of something, then you instantly start thinking about that specific thing. So I turned around to find myself looking out the back of the house, through the window.
Suddenly I saw something hurtle at it and smash straight through, it was a brick! Then a man dressed in a black and white suit dived through the window. My instincts made me drop to the floor, hidden away from the sight of the window, away from the stranger in my house.
I had to do something; someone or something had just warned me about this very thing, and now I needed to prepare myself for what was to come. I made a plan. It wasn't a good plan, but it was a plan. I hid behind a door with my fists clenched ready to attack

if needed. My veins were pumping with adrenaline. I heard the footsteps get closer and then I saw the tip of a black shoe appear around the corner of the doorway. On the spur of the moment I jumped out and swung at the man with my right fist, catching him under his left eye. But then he pulled out a gun! I raised my leg and kicked him in the gut, which made him drop his weapon in agony and weakness. Suddenly, I heard the sound of wood cracking. The back of my head stung as everything started to turn black and my legs collapsed beneath me. I had been knocked out.

When I woke I was in the same place as before and it took me a while to figure out what had happened. As I pulled myself up I tried to recollect what the hell happened here. Then I remembered the letter and the brick and the man. I then realised that I wasn't alone in the house. I listened out for anything peculiar, but there was nothing. Had I dreamt this? Did I make it all up? My head was swimming with both pain and questions, which don't mix very well. I decided to look back at the note. I looked at the childish/rushed handwriting and then I saw the faintest words printed on the back.

I flipped the paper over to reveal a set of instructions. They said:

'You are about to be killed, but not if I can help it.

Follow my instructions.

Step One: Hide this note.

Step Two: Hide yourself.

Step Three: Wait.

Step Four: Check under the table in your kitchen and you will find a bag, it will have money in it and that is for you. It's up to you to decide what to use it for but use it wisely.

Good Luck. From ???'

Well, the first three steps seemed useless to me now. So this person just saved my life by the looks of things, but who; and why were these people trying to kill me?

Then the next thing came to mind, money. I ran into the kitchen to find a Nike sports bag laid under the table. I tore it open to find stacks of notes inside. I had a grin like a child on Christmas morning.

My money problems had been solved, but who was the person who gave it to me?

I'm grateful to be alive, thanks to the letter.

About the Incident

Paul Gledhill

Jim opened the front door of his house and looked out, past his blue ford escort, to the mailbox at the end of his driveway. Still inwardly groaning at this attempt to seem American, he noticed the arm on the mailbox was raised. This was unusual both because it was raised (the postman normally refused to raise it) and also the unusual time that the mail arrived. Jim took his six-foot, slim frame down the garden to retrieve the mail arrival to which he had been alerted.

Picking the single letter out of the box he noted that there was no stamp on it and the address hand-written. Intriguing.

Once inside, he opened the letter and as he read the hand-written contents a deathly cold chill rose in his veins from his feet upwards. He stared at the page dumbfounded, before reading it again.

1. Tomorrow you will find a six-inch knife in your mailbox.

2. Within the week you will use this to kill Neville Miller

Failure to follow these instructions will result in the "incident" involving your wife becoming public knowledge.

That was it. Simple as that. No signature of course. He looked up at the ceiling in the vague direction of where Margaret was asleep in their bed. The "incident" becoming public knowledge; how could he shame her so? How could he shame himself? His family?.......... But murder? And Neville Miller -although their friendship had waned recently they were so close at one time, how could he possibly harm him?

Needless to say a sleepless night ensued after a day totally consumed in his thoughts. Lying next to Margaret he wondered how he could possibly have the "incident" exposed? After violently wrestling with his conscience he came to a decision!

Maybe there was one way out; if he could find out who was blackmailing him. All the next morning he spied from behind his bedroom curtain, looking to see who came to his mailbox. All morning he stared; then his attention was briefly diverted and when he looked again the mailbox flag was raised! He darted out, heart thumping, and opened the mailbox. It was there! He picked up the knife and quickly hid it under his coat and returned inside.

Coming up with a plan was easy enough. He still had a key to Neville's garage from the days when their friendship had been stronger and Jim used to use the gym equipment in the garage. He knew that Neville still used this equipment as regular as clockwork; 6pm each evening.

Two nights later he seemed to have picked the perfect night. It was raining and so the road was deserted. He quietly let himself into the garage, after slowly and nimbly ducking down below the level of the window as he crept in. At 6.15 he was about to think that his plan had been foiled and was just walking towards the door when Neville appeared.

Neville was taken aback, surprised to see him. Before Jim had time to consider what he was doing, now that Neville was standing in front of him, he attempted to rid himself of all feeling and felt his blood turn cold as he plunged the knife into Neville's chest. Neville stopped motionless, stared at Jim in disbelief, then fell to his knees. Jim still had the presence of mind to pull the knife from the dying man's chest before dashing out of the garage and quickly making his way home along rain-soaked streets. Upon arriving home he closed the door behind him and rested his rain-soaked body against the door as he tried to grasp the enormity of what had just happened.

Before the night was out there was the inevitable knock at the door and Jim was arrested. Initially he tried to deny all knowledge of the incident but when another policeman arrived and pushed the note in front of him he thought he should tell all.

He said that he had no idea who wrote the note.

The policeman looked at him and said that he had the note inspected by a hand-writing expert. "We know that the writing is your own Mr Underwood. Is there anything you want to tell us? Jim sat motionless staring blankly ahead.

"What was the "incident" that this refers to Mr Underwood?"

Jim replied slowly, "My wife had an affair."

The policeman nodded, "Who with?"

"Neville Miller!"

Arthur

Helen Disley

Arthur's hands shook as he waited nervously for the postman. He'd bitten all of his nails down to the quick and the half-empty bottle of Jack Daniels perching precariously on the edge of the mantelpiece suggested all was not well. Arthur was not, ordinarily, a drinker.
The first letter had arrived innocently enough just over two months ago, nestled anonymously between his weekly issue of the Radio Times and a junk mailing from a car insurance company.
Arthur had hummed to himself as he poured tea and buttered his morning toast, before taking his breakfast, his tablets and the post outside to enjoy a leisurely breakfast on his sunny patio. This had always been his favourite place, but it was only in the past few weeks he had really been able to enjoy it, now that Pauline was no longer here to find a seemingly endless succession of pointless jobs designed specifically, he felt, to ruin his day. Now he was free to linger on his beloved bench, and gaze around at the neatly trimmed lawn and immaculate flower beds with a sense of unfettered pride.
Strangely, his thoughts often wandered to Pauline as he sat here, remembering happier times when they had truly loved each other. How it was that such devotion could be pared away over time was a mystery to Arthur. Did all marriages eventually deteriorate to the situation they had found themselves in for the last couple of years, when they shared the same house, ate their meals together, but otherwise led quite separate lives, that is, when he wasn't required to fulfil Pauline's ever-expanding task list? He felt a certain amount of guilt that his main emotion when she passed had been one of immense relief, but now, four months on, he felt

mostly peace, knowing his final few years would be his to live out as he pleased.

That is, until The Letter arrived, inviting him to a general health screening at his local GP surgery. He went along innocently enough, being in excellent health for his age. He'd looked after himself since his heart scare just after his 76th birthday.

Unfortunately one of the blood tests had been abnormal and he had since undergone a number of painful and bewildering hospital tests and procedures to determine just how ill he really was.

Arthur was not afraid of dying. He had had a few days now to consider the consequences of a 'bad outcome'. Mostly he felt a huge sense of injustice! He had worked hard his entire life, put up with his unsatisfying marriage, for reasons which now escaped him, and now, when he finally had time to look after number one, it was in great danger of being snatched away before he had even had a chance to fully appreciate it.

He had spent this weekend in a state of heightened anxiety, dreading the day when the final results of all of those degrading tests would arrive. His consultant had told him to expect one of two outcomes, neither of them positive. The first was a slow decline towards the inevitable. Not altogether a welcome situation but one at least in which he would have time to put his life in order, make peace with his daemons and prepare himself for whatever came next. The second outcome would summon him back for immediate surgery, followed by weeks of painful chemotherapy, radiotherapy, possible further surgery and an extremely uncertain future.

He was shaken out of his morose ponderings by the distinctive sound of a single letter being pushed through the mailbox. There was a short pause, during which Arthur imagined the trajectory of the envelope as it dropped silently towards the door mat, followed by a faint slither as the letter landed, bounced and slid a few inches along the highly polished floor.

Arthur took a deep breath and went to retrieve the letter. He held the envelope against his chest for a few seconds, willing the contents to be his discharge letter, then he slid a single finger under the flap, ripped open the envelope and stared at the words on the unwelcome letter.

As he slid to the ground he released the letter and it floated to the floor alongside him, coming to rest against his leg and revealing the words he did not want to see – *"Please arrive at the ward before 8:30am and bring with you the following items....."*

Letters to Rainbow

Nessie Wilkinson

Solving their problems was easier said than done.

How much of this could that "nice social services officer", Ms. Brooklyn, take? Perhaps she was already wilting under the pressure of keeping the Fendersons' lives normal. Well, as normal as a family could be where the son was called Pig (his older brother chose the name) and the second daughter Fairy Bluebell Wishes (her older sister chose the name; the family shortened it to Fairy). Not surprisingly, Ms. Brooklyn's husband suggested that the family change to a different social services officer as it would be "fun to see them try and tame this... unusual family".
Felicity – the mother – was oblivious to Mr. Brooklyn's insult to her family; although she did indeed dislike "that not nice Mr. Brooklyn". The other assorted family members who were outraged about this were: Rainbow (first daughter); Ally (cousin); Sinead (mother to Felicity, i.e. Grandma) and Bob (brother to George, the father, who was generally annoyed by pretty much anything). So, strawberry-blonde hair swishing, the only normal child of Felicity and George, began the chores. As the eldest, she was required to do all of them, as her parents didn't understand how important they were. Rainbow was the eldest in the house at the moment, as well as the eldest of the children, because her parents were talking about a fifth baby downtown in a cafe. Back at the house, Rainbow found a letter in the mailbox. It read:

Dear Rainbow,
I am sorry to say but I heard that your mum has... oh I can barely write it, she has... she has... decided to move you out to London.
This house in Kent just can't fit you anymore. Remember, choose

your own house! Don't let your mum choose for you. Well, you are 19 after all!
Lots of Love
Aunt Casey

Staring in surprise at the salmon-pink paper, Rainbow's large emerald-green eyes widened with shock and pleasure. Half a millisecond later, she was running into the study and was at the computer searching for houses. Looking for a spacious house in bohemian Crouch End, Rainbow performed a classic crazy Fenderson move and started to call her parents, Aunt Casey, the letting agent, her boyfriend, her university head and the taxi service all at once.
"LONDON HERE I COME!!!!" she cried.
"Trying to sleep here! Yes, I know its 3pm," came a voice from the flat above.
Some say: "the luck of the Irish", but this family believed in "the luck of the crazy-Fenderson-action". Rainbow's biggest wish came true. The letting agent gave her the house £100 cheaper per week than advertised, her parents cursed Aunt Casey for ruining the chance to pick Rainbow's house, Brad (Rainbow's boyfriend) agreed to move in with her, the university head told her the new route she would take and the taxi would arrive at 3:15. Everyone was there to see her off as she packed a few possessions and was lead into the taxi by Brad. All the rest of her stuff was to be mailed the next day.
At 5pm, the taxi stopped in front of the new house. Its sloping sea-blue walls set off the ridged white roof to perfection. The door matched it all and each snug little window had its own place. Glass doors opened up to a delightful wide garden with a ready-made trampoline. All the furniture was courtesy of Aunt Casey who loved Rainbow the most (don't tell!). Sitting breathlessly on a sofa Rainbow sighed with delight. The next day, she decided to complete a few chores. Then, she looked inside the mailbox and opened (another) letter.

A Man Finds a Letter

Janet Wolfenden

A man finds a letter in his mailbox. This surprised him, wasn't everything done on the internet nowadays? Pay a bill? Send birthday greetings? Catch up with friends – wherever in the world they were? Internet! He didn't even realise that the post service still operated.

He took it inside, handling it reverently almost like a new-born. Setting it down, balanced against the salt and pepper pots on the kitchen table, he turned to the kettle and filled it ("always from the cold tap, darling, not the hot") and set it to boil whilst assembling the cup, tea bag, milk and spoon. Good heavens, a letter! For ME!

He was surprised he wasn't in a rush to open it. It was a thing of paper and gum, the envelope, that enclosed a message that was totally private and had been carried carefully by the sender to a mailbox somewhere, been collected and sorted, and the final trip by liveried delivery was almost an honour. In the whole process only the sender and the receiver (himself) would ever know the contents – unlike the internet, which by all accounts was hacked and copied and spied on by governments around the globe looking for antagonists to their perfect utopian dream.

He couldn't even remember the last time HE wanted to buy a stamp. Last time he was in a Post Office even? Maybe Christmas – to buy emergency milk?

His darling wife (may she rest in peace) would have ripped it open on the doorstep – anxious to discover the contents. She even kept all the old pizza menus, for heaven's sake, "Just in case, darling, we ever need to entertain in an emergency." The emergency never came, of course, but it didn't put her off. "You NEVER know, darling!"

He sipped the tea – still too hot to drink – and mulled over who he might know that would send such a communiqué. ("Honestly, darling, 'communiqué'? Who uses these words any more?") His son lived in America, the Gulf coast of Florida to be precise, and he was mostly wont to use SKYPE over the internet (such a small world we have now), usually to try to persuade his dad to leave the sulky wet climes of Manchester and come and live it up in the sunny world of holiday resorts and retirement homes. "Dad, you could sell up and buy a home TWICE as big and still have half your money left." His friend Pete would have said he was a fool for not going. Pete the globe-trotting amateur drag racer who took an accident on-track in the US as par for the course and bounced back the next year, to put the fear of UK into the hearts of the American participants in the ET category "over-the-counter" motorcycles.

Pete? No, Pete kept in touch via the huge engine that was Facebook. Even when he was hospitalised after the crash, updates were on Facebook so that everyone could watch and comment on his progress.

Janet. Yes, it was probably from Janet, his sister, a Cystic Fibrosis sufferer like himself and who consequently tended not to visit ("Too much risk of cross-infection, bro"), but would normally email him – apart from when she placed a photograph on her Facebook page – for anything from trivia to an ultimate life-changing plan... No, it wouldn't be Janet.

Sighing, he got up and helped himself to a biscuit. The ginger-furred cat he shared house with ("Darling, you don't OWN a cat, the cat owns you!") crashed through the cat-flap like the hounds of hell were behind it, then sat and had a furious wash in the middle of the kitchen floor. No doubt it had lost the argument with the new neighbourhood black-and-white ("I heard they were called 'Tuxedo' cats, darling") tom cat. "Face it, Grumpy" he said out loud "you're old and past it and might as well watch Spring Watch on the Beeb than try your luck with the birds outside!"

Still didn't answer the question about the origins of the envelope though, did it? There wasn't even a post-mark like there used to be in the old days, from where the stamp had been cancelled with red wavy lines at the sorting office. The special non-peelable stamps did away with that clue.

It was still there, up against the condiments. Might as well open it.

"CONGRATULATIONS!

You have won 1ˢᵗ prize in the novel contest 'A man finds a letter in his mailbox'..."

Scenes of Love

Paul Weston

It had never happened before. This was the first time ever. There had always been respect, love, care. Of course every couple argue, but she was entirely devoted to him. What had happened to them to drive him like this? Bella looked from the pictures she had taken from the envelope straight into the eyes of her husband sitting across the narrow table from her, then back to the pictures.

Ironically he had picked up the envelope this morning. It was addressed to Bella. He'd popped it unthinkingly in the usual place on the mantelpiece, before tootling off to ... who knows where. Yes. Who knows, indeed? He'd said he was off to work, the gym at lunchtime and would be back later on at an unspecified time as he had to meet a new client. So many nights of meeting clients recently. It had started as the odd one or two nights every couple of weeks last autumn, but then gradually ramped up over the course of the year. And it has come to this - this C5 envelope with these disgusting pictures.

There *she* was on the first one. Kissing him, her long, dark hair blowing slightly across his face, her hand caressing his chest. That woman had been her closest friend for so many years. *That woman*. The acid in that single statement could have etched glass. Why? She moved to the next picture; a more explicit scene. Then another picture and another; more and more grotesque and heart wrenching as she went through them.

There was no indication of who had sent the pictures. A label had been stuck on, printed not hand written, askew in the middle of the envelope. No postmark or stamp. The envelope had obviously been hand delivered. Not even a note. She looked at the back of the pictures. They were date and time-stamped, the most recent was yesterday at 12:43. Why?

"Why?" she asked, holding the pictures up in front of his face.

"Did I do something wrong? Did I not look after you? Love you? Cook for you? Clean for you? Pick you up when you were down?"

More tears. She gripped the pictures, crushing triangular creases into them and looked back up at him, wiping the tears from her face on the sleeve of her cardigan.

His big, rubbery, lugubrious head just seemed to hang there, a slight look of surprise on his face. A fat, lazy tear rolled down the tracery of lines and creases beside his bulbous nose until it reached his big lip where it paused deciding what to do next. His bottom lip trembled slightly, dislodging the halted tear, causing it to continue its journey down to his lightly stubbled chin, lodging there instead. His eyes widened and lips parted a little more, as if he would speak. A saliva strand glistened between the yellowed, slightly bucked teeth. A stuttering sigh passed his lips. Then his face returned to its previous simpering expression.

Bella looked at him, taking in his sad blue-grey eyes, set widely apart. She read every little line on his face. She studied the burgundy capillaries of his nose, the little blond hairs sprouting from its bridge to its tip. Then her eyes slipped up to the receding red, curly extravagance on top of his head, showing the odd white strand here and there.

Her gaze returned to those eyes. He blinked his heavy lids, a nervous reaction, the grey bags beneath wobbling ever so slightly. One of his contacts had slipped slightly.

"He won't be able to see properly," Bella thought to herself.

"No. That's silly!" she said, sadness clouding her face. She reached over and pulled the kitchen knife from the bubbling wound in his throat.

Red Dress

Seahwa Won

It was from Greg. Whenever there is a new case from a client he always puts two letters in my mailbox. One is an instruction about the venue and time to meet the client, and the other one is the original letter from the client. This case was about the client's dead daughter, Xinru. According to the letter, there was an accidental fire in Xinru's apartment last year. But the client, Xinru's parents, suspected her boyfriend as the murderer. The two letters were as follows.

Jon,
The client will wait for you in *Opposite* cafe in Manchester Piccadilly at 3 p.m.
See original letter (enclosed).

Dear Mr Savage

You have been recommended to us as a private detective by our family friend. We have been through a hard time since last August and hope you'll be able to help us. My daughter, Xinru, was a lovely and clever lady. Her dream was about to come true but all of sudden it was gone. She was offered an assistant professorship and moved to Manchester last August. Teaching was her dream so we all were very happy and excited. And we also hoped she could settle down well in the new place.
However, we received a call from the police who had identified Xinru dead at home. They said the cause of death was a gas explosion during cooking. But we are writing this letter to you to reinvestigate this case. Fire fighters were dispatched and arrived

at the scene within three minutes according to the report, but the fire had already swallowed the kitchen and Xinru. Apparently the gas hose had become partially disconnected and the gas was leaking. It exploded sometime after she started cooking. But we believe Xinru was murdered by her boyfriend. There are two reasons why we doubt him.

First, her face and hair were extremely clean considering the nature of the fire incident. In particular no damage was found to her respiratory organs. We think this means she was already laying facedown on the floor, dead or dying, at the time before the fire started. Second, she was wearing a red dress. She usually wore black or grey clothes even though her field of study was fashion design. She hated red. Traditionally the colour red symbolises good luck in our country and so it is very popular. But due to many reasons she was struggling to live in China. That was the main reason she left her home country and went to the UK to start a new life. But she was wearing a red dress when the tragedy happened.

We noticed something very weird in photos she posted online. When with her boyfriend, David, she invariably wore red clothes. We think that that is because red is David's favourite colour. He is a huge football fan and the colour red is his team's colour. However, David told the police that he was not near Xinru's flat on the evening of the accident and had an alibi. We are sure that David is telling a lie. The police have already closed the case, but we sincerely hope you will be able to reinvestigate it.

Best regards
Duo Zhang
17 July 2014

Jon put the two letters in the envelope and started smoking. It was a ritual he enjoyed before commencing a new case.

Thirty Pieces of Silver

Paul Gledhill

Jude pressed "disconnect" on his mobile and placed it on the table. Inhaling deeply he tried to grasp the enormity of what he had agreed to. After a few minutes his mobile pinged alerting him to an incoming e-mail. He expertly navigated to his mailbox and opened the e-mail headed "Instructions".

Thanks for agreeing the proposals.
To recap:
Tonight you go to the pre-planned gathering in the park, our officers will be watching. You identify the ring-leader by kissing him; our officers then swoop in and arrest him. Once the operation is completed successfully, you are given your payment by someone handing you a small bag.
Regards

He sat back, reflecting. This course of action was perfectly acceptable. He was becoming disillusioned with the whole scenario. It all seemed to be losing its focus. Maybe the final straw was that perfume incident. It was bad enough that the woman had actually thrown that expensive perfume over the leader; but when he actually condoned it! Surely this was the biggest waste of money ever. If he was given the bottle of perfume he could've got a great price from his internet connections and given the money to the poor or just for their own funds.

As self-appointed treasurer for their organisation he opened a spreadsheet on his computer and shook his head, pondering the financial situation. There was never enough money. And tonight presumably a room would be hired for supper; paid for with what exactly? He's no idea about how to promote the business, thought Jude, he talks about things on a global scale but hasn't even got a business plan to promote this locally! Their little group needs some fresh blood in charge if this is to become viable in what may become a competitive market. Yes, completely justified. The greater good.

That evening he drove to the park silently; didn't even have the radio on which was very unusual. He parked up and took the east entrance. He saw a small crowd gathered already, mainly the usual suspects wanting to hear more of the rambling.

He knew what he had come for and so there was no reason to delay, he headed straight for the small gathering congregated near the large oak tree. He headed purposefully to the group looking at the leader who stopped talking and looked straight towards him as he approached. He hated it when he looked at him this way; like he could see straight through him into his mind and, more uncomfortably, his heart.

He walked through the crowd, his path seemed to part before him, and straight to the leader. His intention was just to do the deed, let what would happen happen and leave, but when he got to arms length he stopped. They looked each other directly in the eye.

Finally the leader broke the uneasy silence saying, "Do what you've come to do."

With that Jude said, "Yes, teacher," and kissed his left cheek.

Then he turned away and, as he did so, pandemonium let loose. People suddenly sprang from the shelter of the trees, some with dogs. A helicopter appeared overhead, its searchlight blinding the crowd.

Jude managed to back away and then left the unfolding bedlam and trotted back to his car. Just before he reached it a heavy bag was thrust into his hand, he knew it was the money.

By the time he got home his mood had changed completely and he was very sombre. He thought about what he had done, the look he saw as he walked towards him. Had he handed this man over to his death? A fair trial seemed impossible. He thought back over these last three years. He had certainly seen some amazing things, amazing claims. He couldn't say that anything wrong had happened. All done with best intention, with love. And what would be happening to him now? Jude knew that he could have avoided it. And that look tonight; those words. He saw the bag of uncounted money on the side. Had he really sunk this low? A grief entered his heart like he'd never known, allowing access into the deepest recesses of his soul; he couldn't bear what he saw.

Standing on the chair in the field behind his house he stared at the circle created by the noose. He threw the bag of money just before he jumped. As he did so, on a nearby hill, a man was being nailed to a cross.

Adam and Eve

Stephen Westland

Breakfast was not particularly appetising but she was ravenously hungry after having been out late last night. She gobbled it down greedily and licked every remnant from the inside of the bowl. It tasted a bit like chicken but she had long since given up wondering what it actually was. It was filling, and once you got used to it, it didn't really taste that bad, but she preferred something that she could get her teeth into. She was definitely a girl that liked her meat.

Three weeks ago, when they had been laying together on the bed, one of the last times that Mr B had been able to get up the stairs if she remembered correctly, she had accidentally wet the bed. The most surprising thing about the whole episode was that Mr B did not even seem to notice. Or, if he did, he was too polite to say anything about it, despite the fact that it stank to high heaven. It literally reeked and so she could only assume that Mr B wanted to save her feelings and, embarrassed as she was, she was very grateful for that.

Licking her lips to make sure she had not missed any bits, she heard the envelope flap and the unmistakable sound of a letter slap onto the parquet floor. She raced through to the hall and saw a white manila envelope with writing on the front. Almost certainly it was another letter for Mr B. He was very particular about his letters and she knew she would be in trouble if she damaged it; she had already accidently trodden on it. There was a small mark but no damage done. She was sure that the ink marks on the front of the envelope were letters but to be honest she couldn't really make them out. Really, the letter could have been addressed to anyone for all she knew.

She listened carefully for the sound of snoring from the living room where Mr B had recently been sleeping. Ever since he developed that bad leg, he had been sleeping downstairs now. She would have liked to have slept with Mr B to keep him company, at least in the same room, especially since he had been coughing so much recently, but Mr B complained about her flatulence (he said it woke him up at night). She could hardly tell him it was the brown stuff that he had been buying for meals. Of course, he had said it was all they could afford.

Looking again at the envelope she noticed some of the writing was in red ink. This was normally a sign that the letter was important. Probably it was official and Mr B would want to know about it immediately. In some ways it was quite surprising that the clatter of the letterbox had not woken him up. She pushed the living room door open and wandered in. It was quite dark though she had always had really good night vision. Even when it was so dark that Mr B was groping his way around, she could always see where things were. So even though the curtains were closed and the lights were switched off, she could easily make out the form of Mr B laying flat-out on the couch. She also could not help but notice the smell of urine and hoped that she would not be blamed for that. She softly padded over towards the couch, enjoying the softness of the carpet on her bare feet. Since he was fast asleep she jumped up and sat upon his chest. Despite the fact that she was incredibly delicate, normally it would have woken him up. But it did not. It was not until she curled up so that her face was snuggled under Mr B's chin that she noticed how cold his skin was when, normally, it was extremely warm. It was also strange that his chest was not rising and falling as it usually did. She settled down to sleep, purring deeply, and wondered what was in the envelope.

The Game

John M. Bishop

The letter was waiting for him on Tuesday morning. His imagination flared as he opened it and read, "2:30 pm, Cloudy Bay Roof Terrace, Harvey Nichols; book me a centre table from were I might throw peanuts to the little birds that flock around Knightsbridge".
It was delicious to be rich, with a curious lover to entertain him so; and he smiled ..

At noon she wandered through her wardrobe to consider :- she would need her Alice & Oliver lilac wrap front maxi skirt and a plain white halter top; offset with a chunky black necklace, cream strap heels and a heavy dark wrist bangle.
She ran a foaming bath and soaked a while before dressing carefully and scenting herself in a light mist of *Chance Eau Fraîche*.
The afternoon was warm; she was tall and, as always, attracted gaze as she glided through Chelsea. Her spending became her and the doorman nodded courteously as she entered Harvey's to take the lift to the fifth floor.
The restaurant was, as usual, busy with visitors. The little white wood and metal table was reserved as she'd instructed: a bottle of Krug Brut 1988 waiting in an ice bucket; a single crystal flute sparkling; a small tray of hors d'oeuvres and an ashtray - she always savoured the indulgence of Davidoff slims with lunch.
The table was bang in the centre of a small row at the edge of the terrace overlooking Knightsbridge, with an uninterrupted view of the parade of insanely priced flats opposite. She sat facing them; nodded at the Maitre d'; took the cigarettes from her Gucci shoulder bag and indicated to the waiter to pour champagne.

On the table to her left was a family of French tourists enthusiastically enjoying tea and scones; to her right, two Italian suited Arab businessmen engrossed in spreadsheets and fine wine. She arranged herself as elegantly as possible in the patio chair, lit a Davidoff and - as she smoked - knowingly and indecorously uncrossed her legs.

She relaxed further into the chair. Folds of fabric fell slightly open, exposing her knees and calves; her waxed and moisturised skin shone alluringly to any that might notice; the three cream straps of her patent leather heels glistened in the sun. She was pleased with the effect and surveyed the flats opposite; he would be there, somewhere, observing.

But those who owned property in Knightsbridge value their privacy and the Georgian windows merely reflected her gaze.

It was warm and she fanned languorously with her menu as she finished the cigarette and thoughtfully sipped at the champagne: £498, as the wine - and her beauty - announced, bought a certain quality.

Of course she was obliged to inch the folds of her skirt upwards across her thighs in such a manner as to not attract the attention of the waiters (or anyone else). And as the fabric of the wrap slid slowly aside - she was careful to remain absolutely discreet - the light lilac cotton parted further to reveal the tops of her unimpeachably toned legs and she felt the afternoon sun begin to probe. The day was warm and the champagne sizzled; she reclined luxuriantly, savouring time in this world.

The iPhone surprised her. She deftly slipped the headphones on, hidden behind long, and perfectly straight, blonde hair. "I see you", a soft voice purred into her ears. She listened to his breathing, soft, regular; her eyes half-closed. She had one gift and that gift was imagination; she imagined exceedingly well ..

So, whilst her fellow diners discussed the price of fine jewellery and petrochemicals, she magicked herself into his private view: to feel secret hands tracing her knees; exploring her thighs; opening her sex to a lover's gaze.

And she conjured small kisses on her neck, light caresses across her back, the nudge of a shoe brushing naked calf. Her pulse quickened and she began to redden; quietly; inexorably; but there had to be more. To win at their game she needed just a little more; now.

Until deep-breathing in her ears betrayed his binoculared gaze finally alighting on her thighs, open under the table; her shoes now forcing her splayed feet to arch. She flushed deeply and her long fingers tightened their grip on the thin wooden armrests of the chair, compelling her breasts to rise; pulling her halter top tight. She smiled, imperceptibly shuddered and climaxed; noiselessly.

It truly was a quiet and unobtrusive way to live...

About the Authors

Rasheeda Azam has a MA in Creative Writing from Bath Spa University and writes novels and short stories. She has been published by Commonwealth Writers, University of Maine and the Readers Digest amongst others. She is currently working on a crime novel about a literary agent who is murdered and four people from her past who all had reason to kill her.

John Mark Bishop is Professor of Cognitive Computing at Goldsmiths, where his research explores how interactions between 'neuron and brain'; 'brain and body' and 'body and world' form and shape consciousness. He is married to a Greek Kat with whom he shares a little squark they call Ada.

Helen Disley lives with her husband in County Durham in the UK. She has worked as a research chemist and an information analyst. This is her first attempt at fiction.

Nathan Dunn is 15 years old and lives in Darlington, UK. He enjoys reading and writing short stories and hopes one day to be a screenwriter/journalist.

Debra Fayter is a university researcher by day. By night she performs stand-up comedy. Debra enjoys writing flash fiction and relishes the challenge of telling a compelling story in so few words.

Keith Findlater has had a life-long career in photography with specialisms including cultural heritage, portraiture, computer graphics, archiving and colour research. Brought up in London and living in York, Keith's writing has developed by enrolling on accredited courses in Creative Chronicles, Short Stories and Scriptwriting for Stage, Screen and Radio.

Alexandra Gekousidou was born in Sweden, but currently lives in Greece, where she teaches English and Italian, as her studies were on languages and journalism. Her travels and wandering spirit are transparent in her writing.

Paul Gledhill works as a community nurse in Manchester supporting people who have severe learning disabilities. In recent times has found a renewed vigour for returning to writing.

Suzanne Grinnan might have been a weaver, museum curator, explorer, professional swimmer, or even writer in one of her previous lives. In this, she runs a scientific society by day and spends free time gardening, preserving, and exploring her love of different cultures through their cuisines. A resident of Washington, DC, she shares the vice of seed catalogue lust with her protagonist.

Clay Kindred studied History at Kenyon College. He is a freelance writer, and lives in New York City with his wife Dimitra and son Leo.

Ján Morovič works as a senior colour scientist at Hewlett Packard in Barcelona. He has in excess of a hundred academic publications and paints whenever he can. He lives in Colchester with his wife Karen and sons Jan and Thomas.

Stephen Westland has worked for most of his life as an academic and holds a Professorship at a leading British university. He is also an independent writer and *Mutation*, his first novel, was published in 2014. He lives in Leeds with his wife Jane and his son Tyler.

Paul Weston is a software developer for an NHS Trust in the North of England. This is his first attempt at producing a short story and he seriously enjoyed it (though may have lost some hair trying to compact them down to their required length!).

Nessie Wilkinson is 10 years old and lives in Muswell Hill. She hopes to succeed in the future as a journalist/author as she likes reading and writing.

Janet Wolfenden is a Graphic Designer and Amateur Photographer. She is 54 years old and a Cystic Fibrosis sufferer.

Seahwa Won is undertaking a PhD in design at the University of Leeds. Her interest is colour in design and branding. Her home country is South Korea and where she has worked as a graphic designer.

A Personal Message

We hope you enjoyed this book as much as we enjoyed putting it together.

Engaging with readers and hearing what they think is important to us. If you want to tell us what you think about the book please email us at stephenwestland@gmx.com. However, it is a tough world for independent writers and we need all of the help we can to be successful. So if you enjoyed the book please tell your friends about it and, if you can spare the time, please take a few minutes to enter a review about the book on Amazon. Positive reviews are so important to us.

Stephen Westland and Helen Disley

3rd September 2014

V1.1

Printed in Great Britain
by Amazon